Table of Contents

TRIANGLE OF HEARTS
A TALE OF LOVE, RIVALRY, AND SELF-DISCOVERY

Copyright © 2024

ABOUT THE AUTHOR

BRAIENS Trinidad, originally hailing from the Dominican Republic, is a dynamic literary voice now based in the bustling metropolis of New York City. With a passion for storytelling deeply rooted in his Caribbean heritage, Trinidad brings to life vivid worlds and unforgettable characters in his novels. Captivating readers with its evocative prose and compelling narrative. When he's not immersed in the world of writing, Trinidad enjoys exploring the diverse cultural offerings of New York City and savoring home-cooked Dominican dishes with his family.

CHAPTER 1

CAPTIVATING BEGINNINGS

As Mia and Clara navigated through the crowded gallery, the vibrant canvases weren't the only artworks capturing attention. When Mia first laid eyes on Alex, standing by his striking black-and-white photographs, something in the air seemed to shift. His quick, appreciative glance towards her was fleeting, yet it sent a warm, tingling sensation up her spine. His approach was bold, his handshake firmer than expected, with his fingers lingering just a second longer than necessary. Their interaction was charged with an unspoken intrigue, each laugh and gaze laden with potential.

Later, as Mia drifted towards Jamie, the contrast was palpable. His presence was calming, his smile gentle, drawing her into a quieter corner of the gallery. When he discussed the artwork, his hand lightly touched her elbow, guiding her view to a particular piece he was discussing. It was a subtle gesture resonating deeply with Mia, stirring a sense of closeness she hadn't anticipated. His words were thoughtful, his pauses filled with an inviting warmth that encouraged Mia to share her interpretations, making the art around them feel alive with shared secrets.

The evening took a playful turn when Alex, ever the instigator of spontaneity, challenged Mia to a game of spotting the most unconventional piece in the room. Their quest through the gallery became a lighthearted chase, with Alex playfully blocking her path or darting ahead with a mischievous grin. Each laugh and playful dispute brought them closer, blurring the lines between mere acquaintance and something more flirtatious.

Meanwhile, Mia's mind was a whirlwind of emotions. Mia reflected on the night's encounters as she and Clara settled into a quiet corner with their coffee after the night she had at the gallery. "Clara," she began, her voice tinged with excitement and confusion. The night felt like stepping into a living story. One moment, I'm swept up in Alex's daring world, feeling like anything is possible.

The next, I'm anchored by Jamie's depth, where every word resonates with my soul."

Clara nodded, sipping her coffee thoughtfully. "It sounds like both of them have stirred something in you. It's not just about choosing between excitement and stability, Mia. It's about deciding who makes you feel more alive and like yourself."

Mia pondered Clara's words; her gaze lost in the steam rising from her cup. The night had opened new horizons, and as the city lights flickered outside, mirroring the tumult of her thoughts, she realized that her journey was beginning. This was not just about choosing between two potential lovers but about understanding her heart's desires in the face of contrasting passions.

Mia and Clara continued conversing under the soft glow of the coffee shop's vintage lamps. Each word Clara spoke weaves a tapestry of wisdom and comfort, allowing Mia to unravel the complexities of her feelings in a safe space.

"I'm sure both men have sparked something unique in you," Clara observed, her voice a soothing balm to a conflicted soul. With Alex, it's as if you're dancing on the edges of a thrilling cliff—exhilarating, maybe a bit dangerous. With Jamie, dislike sinking into a deep, serene lake, where the world seems clearer, more profound."

Mia nodded, absorbing Clara's analogies. The imagery helped her visualize her emotions as tangible landscapes, each evoking distinct sensations and allure. "Like being torn between a storm and a symphony," Mia mused aloud, her fingers tracing the rim of her coffee cups, exactly! "Claraexclaimed, her eyes bright with understanding. "But remember, Mia, the choice isn't just about the storm's excitement or the symphony's harmony. It's about where you can sing your song and be your truest self."

The resonance of Clara's words struck a deep chord within Mia. As the night deepened, the coffee shop began to empty, the barista quietly stacking chairs and wiping down tables. The world outside seemed to hold its breath, waiting for a decision, yet inside, the warm sanctuary of the café offered her a momentary reprieve from the urgency of choice.

Feeling a newfound clarity beginning to emerge, Mia took a deep breath, her decision slowly crystallizing. She realized that her heart was not just choosing between two men but between different versions of herself that each man brought to light.

With a gentle sigh, Mia turned to Clara, her expression of resolve mixed with gratitude. "Clara, talking to you tonight has opened my eyes. I need to think about who brings joy into my life and who nurtures my soul."

Clara smiled, reaching across the table to squeeze hands. "Take all the time you need, Mia. This isn't just about choosing who you want to be with. It's about choosing who you want to be."

As they left the café, the crisp air seemed to echo the clarity of Mia's thoughts. The city, with its myriad lights and shadows, mirrored the complexity of Mia's emotions, yet she felt a steadiness within her, a sense that the path ahead, though uncertain, was hers to choose.

As they walked, Mia's mind replayed the events of the evening, each interaction with Alex and Jamie taking on new significance. She knew the days ahead would bring challenges and revelations, but for the first time in a long while, she felt equipped to face them, fortified by the insights gained from their late-night talks' quiet refuge.

With the cityscape stretching out before them, Clara and Mia continued their walk, their steps lit, their spirits lifted by the promise of a new beginning.

As Mia and Clara made their way down the quiet, lamplit street, the city around them seemed to pulse with a life of its own, each light a beacon guiding Mia through her tangled thoughts. The evening's revelations opened avenues of self-reflection that Mia hadn't anticipated when she first stepped into the gallery. As the night drew close, her mind was alight with possibilities.

"She thinks about choices," Clara mused as they paused at a crosswalk, the light flickering from red to green, " that they are often scarier in anticipation than in reality. Whatever you decide will lead you to where you need to be."

Mia smiled at her friend, grateful for the serene wisdom flowing effortlessly from her. "You make it sound so simple," she replied, her tone light but her eyes reflecting the depth of her introspection.

"It can be, sometimes," Clara said with a shrug as they resumed walking. " Remember to listen to your heart as much as your head. They both have important things to say."

As they reached the apartment building, the towering structure cast long shadows over the street, and the architecture was a stark reminder of the endless possibilities. Here, at the threshold of her home, the night's experiences crystallized into a determination to explore the choices between Alex and Jamie and her evolving desires and dreams.

"I think I'm going to take a day just to be alone tomorrow," Mia declared, her voice firm with newfound resolve. "I need to let all this settle, maybe find a quiet corner of the city just to think."

Clara nodded, her smile supportive. "That sounds like a perfect plan. And who knows? A little solitude may be just what you need to see things more clearly.

They hugged in a long, tight embrace that spoke volumes of their bond. "Thank you, Clara," Mia said as they parted. "For everything."

"Anytime," Clara replied, stepping back. It's all me if you need anything, okay?"

With a final wave, Mia turned and entered the lobby of her building, the familiar space a comforting end to an evening full of unexpected turns. As she ascended the elevator, her thoughts began drifting towards tomorrow. She envisioned a quiet park, the gentle rustle of leaves, and a notebook to pour her thoughts into.

CHAPTER 2

CHASING THRILLS

As the city's heartbeat thudded in sync with the fading evening light, Mia's phone buzzed alive with an unexpected message from Alex. The screen lit up with an invitation that sparked curiosity: "Adventure tonight? Trust me, you won't want to miss this." Her fingertips hovered over the keyboard, the thrill of spontaneity tingling at her spine. With excitement and a dash of recklessness, she typed, "I'm in."

Minutes later, the roar of a motorcycle broke the stillness outside her apartment. Alex, clad in a leather jacket that seemed to meld with the night, greeted her with a helmet in hand and a mischievous grin. "Ready for something unforgettable?" he asked, his voice a thrilling promise.

Climbing onto the back of the motorcycle, Mia felt a rush of wind and freedom as they sped through the neon-lit streets. The city blurred into streaks of color and light, each turn and twist sharpening the electric buzz that filled the air between them. Alex's confidence was infectious, and his ease on the bike made Mia throw her usual caution to the winds. She laughed; the sound lost in the rush of air as they weaved through the nighttime traffic.

Their destination was an old, seemingly abandoned warehouse in a forgotten town. Alex led her inside, where the dim exterior gave way to a cavernous space illuminated by an array of eccentric art pieces. It was an avant-garde installation, hidden away from the prying eyes of the mainstream. Sculptures made from reclaimed materials stood as silent sentinels and abstract paintings danced on the walls in vibrant, chaotic hues.

Alex watched as she took it all in, his gaze intense yet playful. "This place," he began, his voice echoing slightly in the vast room, "is where the unbridled spirit of art lives. Each piece tells a story of breaking free, of daring to defy expectations."

Mia felt a connection to the raw, untamed energy of the art around her. It was as if each piece beckoned her to shed her reservations and embrace a world of uncharted possibilities. She turned to Alex, seeing him as a guide to this hidden gem and a fellow seeker of life's exhilarating moments.

Their exploration became a game of discovery. Alex would describe a piece in vivid detail, then challenge Mia to uncover deeper meanings, his insights sparking lively debates that bubbled with laughter and intellectual sparks. His hand occasionally brushed hers, each contact sending a jolt of awareness through her. The playful banter, the exchange of ideas, and the thrill of new experiences melded into a night of exhilarating exploration.

As they stood before a particularly striking sculpture—a maze of twisted metal and soft, glowing lights—Alex's voice softened. "Sometimes," he said, "you find paths in life you never expected to take. And sometimes, those paths find you."

Mia felt the weight of his words, realizing how this unexpected night altered her perception of art and Alex. He was no longer just a charming acquaintance; he was becoming a catalyst for her to explore the parts of herself she often kept restrained.

Their conversation drifted to dreams and desires, the sculpture shifting shadows over their faces as they shared pieces of themselves that were usually guarded. Mia divulged her aspirations, fears, and the thrill of the unknown that the evening had inspired.

The warehouse, with its atmosphere of defiance and freedom, seemed to encapsulate the essence of their outing—a shared escape from the mundane, a mutual challenge to the constraints of everyday life. As the night deepened, so did their connection, each revelation and shared laugh drawing them closer in a dance of budding intimacy.

Finally, as the early morning hours hinted at their approach, Alex offered Mia a ride back. The streets were now deserted and softly lit by streetlights as the city had grown quieter. The ride back was more peaceful, a contemplative journey that contrasted with their earlier exuberance. Mia leaned closer to Alex, her thoughts a whirlwind of emotions stirred by the night's adventures.

Upon reaching her apartment, the chill of the dawn made Mia shiver, and Alex draped his jacket over her shoulders. "Tonight was about sharing a piece of my world with you," he said, his voice earnestly. "I hope it meant as much to you as it did to me."

Mia nodded, her heart full. "It did, Alex. It did." As he drove away, the sound of the motorcycle fading into the morning, Mia felt a profound shift within her. The Adventure showed her a new side of Alex and rekindled her spirit of Adventure and her desire to live boldly.

As she entered her apartment, the quiet felt welcoming. Mia knew that sleep would be elusive, her mind replaying every moment, every sensation of the night.

There was a peaceful anticipation within her, a readiness for whatever surprises life might throw her way next. The night she had opened new horizons, not just in her relationship with Alex but in her journey of self-discovery.

In the solitude of her home, Mia sat by the window, the first light of dawn casting gentle patterns on the floor. She penned her thoughts, feelings, and vivid impressions of the night. This wasn'tjust another chapter in her life; it was an awakening to a world where she could be fearless and chase life's thrills with someone who challenged her to embrace her true self.

As she wrote, her thoughts briefly wandered to Jamie. How would he fit into this new equation she was drafting with Alex? The question lingered, a quiet note in the symphony of her exhilarating night. But for now, she savored the afterglow of Adventure, ready to see where this newfound courage would take her next.

Energized by the night's revelations, Mia continued to document her thoughts, the pen gliding effortlessly across the pages of her journal. Each word she wrote was imbued with the residual excitement of the evening, crafting a narrative that was both a reflection and a discovery. The Adventure with Alex had peeled back layers of her daily routine, revealing a vibrant tapestry of risk and spontaneity that resonated deeply with her burgeoning spirit.

Mia's contemplation shifted toward the future as the sky transitioned from night's deep indigo to dawn's softer hues. The adventures of the evening had planted seeds of daring in her heart, inspiring a longing for more experiences that pushed the boundaries of her comfort zone. She pondered the possibilities ahead, each path infused with the promise of new challenges and growth.

The journal pages filled steadily, a testament to Mia's unfolding journey. She wrote about the thrills of the motorcycle ride and how the city appeared different from the back of Alex's bike, racing through the night. She captured the essence of the warehouse art installation, where each piece challenged conventional aesthetics and provoked thought. Mia explored the significance of each moment through her words, finding deeper meanings in the night's escapades.

Mia set aside her journal as the first rays of morning light filtered through her window, casting long shadows across the floor. Her mind was alight with thoughts, yet a serene calm enveloped her. It was as if the night's adventures had cleared a mental fog, sharpening her focus, and deepening her resolve.

In this quiet morning hour, Mia realized the value of such unexpected experiences in shaping her perceptions. They were not just escapes from the mundane but pivotal moments that could steer the course of her life. The excitement Alex brought into her life was intoxicating but enlightening, revealing her hidden desires for a less ordinary life.

With a stretch and a yawn, Mia prepared for the day ahead. Though sleep had been scant, her energy was buoyed by anticipation for what lay ahead. She decided to walk in the nearby park, where the city's pulse was softened by the rustling of leaves and the gentle paths winding through greenery. Here, she could process the whirlwind of feelings and thoughts from the night before in peace.

As she walked, the park was coming alive with the early risers—joggers, dog walkers, and others who found solace in the morning calm. Mia's mind replayed the conversations with Alex, his words, his laughter, the touch of his hand. Each memory brought a smile to her lips and a flutter to her heart. Yet, in the backdrop of her exhilarating memories with Alex, the image of Jamie occasionally surfaced—his thoughtful demeanor, his reflective gaze. The contrast between Alex's vivid canvas of life and Jamie's deep, serene waters was striking.

In the solitude of the park, Mia grappled with these contrasting desires. Alex's world was vibrant colors and bold strokes, while Jamie's was about depth and texture. Each man offered something different, something valuable. How could she choose between the thrill of spontaneity and the comfort of depth?

Lost in thought, Mia didn't notice a small, playful dog darting towards her until it was playfully tugging at the edge of her jacket. She laughed, the sound mingling with the morning air, and knelt to greet the enthusiastic dog. Its owner, a friendly older woman, apologized and struck up a conversation. They talked about the park, the city, and the little escapes that made life interesting. This interaction was simple yet warm and grounded Mia. It reminded her that joy could be found in unexpected encounters, small moments, and grand adventures.

By the time Mia left the park, her thoughts were clearer. She recognized that her journey wasn't just about choosing between Alex and Jamie; it was about understanding her needs and desires, about crafting a life that was as rich and varied as the experiences that shaped her. The park offered a respite and a lens to view her situation anew.

Mia returned home with newfound clarity and a plan to explore her feelings further. She was ready to face whatever the day would bring, equipped with the insights from her morning reflections.

Filled with reflections from her morning in the park, Mia returned to her apartment, her mind teeming with insights and a rejuvenated spirit. She brewed herself a cup of coffee, the rich aroma filling the kitchen, grounding her in the moment. With her journal on the table, she captured the last threads of thought from her morning walk, each word a deliberate step toward clarity.

As the city awakened around her, the usual noises of sounds drifting through her open window, Mia considered the day ahead. The contrast between Alex's spontaneous zest for life and Jamie's introspective calm continued to play on her mind. She needed more than fleeting moments and reflective mornings to make the right decision. It was clear to her now that she needed to dive deeper into both men's worlds to truly understand her heart.

Later that morning, while Mia was sketching in her living room, her phone chimed with a new message. Jamie invited her to a quaint bookshop for an afternoon, where he hosted a discussion on modern poetry. The event, he suggested, would be a peaceful way to spend the day, a stark contrast to the exhilarating night with Alex. Mia accepted, intrigued by the opportunity to step into Jamie's world, a place of thoughtful dialogue and reflective silence.

As Mia prepared to meet Jamie, she chose her outfit with care, opting for something that mirrored the serenity of the occasion—a soft, flowing dress paired with comfortable flats. She glanced at her reflection, noting how different she felt gearing up for an afternoon of poetry compared to the exhilarating ride with Alex. Each event pulled different strings in her heart, each a unique color on her emotional palette.

Meeting Jamie at the bookshop, Mia was enveloped in a world of quiet intellect. The shelves were lined with tomes of all sizes, each spine a gateway to another world, another mind. Jamie's demeanor was calm, his excitement more subdued but no less genuine as he guided her through his favorite sections, occasionally pulling down a volume to read a particularly moving passage.

The poetry discussion was a small, intimate group, and Mia was drawn into the nuanced interpretations of the poems. Jamie's insights revealed layers she hadn't noticed, his gentle enthusiasm infectious. As they discussed, Mia appreciated the depth of connection possible through shared thoughts and ideas. Jamie's presence was like a steady flame, warming her with its glow of reliability and intellectual connection.

After the discussion, they shared a quiet meal in a nearby café, their conversation flowing from literature to personal philosophies. Mia found comfort in Jamie's company, the ease of the interaction, and the shared silences that felt just as communicative as their discussions.

As the day ended, Mia felt peaceful contentment. She thanked Jamie for a wonderful afternoon, and his smile in response was both shy and pleased. Mia returned to the contrast between her experiences with Alex and Jamie as they parted. Each man offered a different facet of life, each appealing and valuable.

Walking home, Mia knew that her journey of discovery was not yet complete. Both experiences had opened her eyes to new possibilities, leading her to question what she truly wanted in a partner reflecting on her experiences, hoping to find some direction in the jumble of her emotions.

Her footsteps echoed on the pavement as she returned, the city's twilight hues casting long shadows. Tomorrow's solitude would be crucial, a pause in the whirl of her interactions with Alex and Jamie. As Mia entered her apartment, closing the door behind her, she felt a profound appreciation for the complexity of her emotions, knowing that each step and decision brought her closer to understanding her own heart.

CHAPTER 3

QUIET INTENSITY

The brisk air of the evening wrapped around Mia as she approached the venerable facade of the old city library, its stone walls bathed in the warm glow of street lamps. A sense of anticipation fluttered in her chest. It was the second time she agreed to meet with Jamie a week after their first date, mingling with the serene calm that the library exuded, Jamie had chosen this spot not just for its vast collection of books but for its secluded nooks, perfect for their private poetry reading.

As she pushed open the heavy wooden door, the familiar scent of aged paper and polished wood enveloped her, instantly soothing her senses. The library was a world away from the pulsating energy of her night with Alex, offering a sanctuary of thought and reflection instead. Jamie was already there, standing amidst the towering shelves, a slim volume of poetry in his hand. His warm and inviting smile was like a beacon as he waved her over.

"Ah, Mia, you're here," Jamie greeted her, his voice a soft echo in the library's vast, peaceful expanse. I thought we'd start here, in the poetry section. There's something about these verses that transcends time and space."

As they settled into a secluded corner, the gentle rustle of pages turning nearby only added to the ambiance. Jamie handed her the book he had been holding—a collection of romantic poetry from the Victorian era. His finger traced the lines of a particularly moving sonnet, his touch gentle on the aged paper.

"Listen to this," he began, his voice a whisper, "'Love is not love which alters when its alteration finds.' Shakespeare knew the constancy true affection demands. What do you think he meant by that?"

Mia leaned closer, her mind engaging with the words as her senses soaked up the tranquility of their surroundings. The intimacy of the moment, coupled with the intellectual stimulation of their discussion, wove a compelling tapestry that appealed deeply to her. Her response was thoughtful, a reflection of her own experiences and the desire for steadfast love.

Their conversation meandered through various poets and eras, each poem sparking new thoughts and revelations. Jamie's insights were profound, showing a deep sensitivity and understanding of human emotions and relationships. His ability to connect literary themes to their personal lives made Mia appreciate the layers of his personality more than ever.

Their surroundings seemed to draw them closer as the evening progressed—physically and emotionally. The library, with its dim lighting and the soft background murmur of other guests, created a bubble that felt removed from the outside world. It was in this bubble that Mia found herself more drawn to Jamie than she had anticipated. His presence was calming yet electrifying in its subtlety.

During a pause in their reading, Jamie reached out to tuck a stray lock of hair behind Mia's ear. The gesture was tender, charged with an unspoken affection that sent a shiver down Mia's spine. His touch lingered longer, bridging the gap between intellectual attraction and budding romantic interest.

"Sometimes," Jamie said, breaking the charged silence, "I find that words give us a way to express what's hidden deep within us. They're not just marks on a page but keys to unlocking our deepest emotions."

Mia nodded, her heart beating a tad quicker, her breath catching slightly in her throat. The depth of the connection they forged through the poetry and their discussions was unexpectedly moving. She opened up more about her dreams, past relationships, and aspirations than usual on a second date.

As they closed the book and prepared to leave, the emotional stakes of their growing connection became apparent. Outside the safety of the library's walls, the real world awaited its demands and decisions. The contrast between the night's tranquility and the complexity of her feelings for Jamie and Alex loomed large in Mia's mind.

Walking out into the cool night air, Jamie offered her his jacket, noticing the slight shiver on her shoulders. The gesture was protective, a silent affirmation of his care. As they walked, their conversation turned to plans for another meeting, both aware that the connection they were exploring was something neither wanted to rush.

Reaching her doorstep, Jamie leaned in, his eyes searching hers for permission, which she silently granted. Their kiss was gentle, a perfect end to an evening of shared vulnerabilities and quiet intensities. It wasn't just a physical connection but an emotional promise of more to come.

As Jamie departed, Mia leaned against her door, her mind a whirlwind of emotions. Tonight, she had deepened her feelings for Jamie, complicating her romantic landscape even further. She was drawn to his intellect and emotional depth, which vividly contrasted with Alex's vibrant spontaneity.

Mia knew the next chapter of her journey would involve deeper self-exploration. She needed to understand her heart's desires more fully to navigate the intricate dance of her feelings toward both men. Tomorrow, she planned to take a long walk in the city park, hoping the open spaces would help her clarify her tangled emotions.

Mia is standing on the threshold of profound emotional discoveries, her heart pulled in different directions by two distinctly different men, each offering a unique love and connection.

As she stepped inside, Mia's apartment felt unusually quiet, the echo of her footsteps a stark reminder of the solitude that awaited her. The contrast between the day's quiet intensity with Jamie and the stillness of her own space was palpable. She found herself missing the soft murmur of the library and the gentle cadence of Jamie's voice as he recited poetry. It was a missing piece that seemed to fill a void she hadn't known existed.

Standing by the window, Mia watched the city lights flicker like distant stars, casting a delicate glow over the urban landscape. The evening with Jamie had left an imprint on her heart, a warmth that lingered in the cool night air. Yet, the thrill of her adventures with Alex also tugged at her spirit, a vibrant call to embrace the unknown with open arms.

She poured herself a glass of wine, the ruby liquid reflecting the dim light as she swirled it gently. The wine was a fine blend; its complex layers are a perfect metaphor for her current emotional state—rich, nuanced, and slightly unpredictable. Mia pondered over her feelings as she sipped, trying to discern the threads of her emotions woven so intricately together.

Her journal lay on the table, its pages waving for more words and revelations. With a deep breath, Mia began to write, her pen moving fluidly across the paper. She wrote of the library's serenity, the poetry's thrill, and how each word seemed to resonate with something deep within her. She wrote of Jamie's thoughtfulness, gentle respect for her opinions, and safety in his presence.

Yet, as she wrote, her mind drifted to Alex—his daring spirit, infectious enthusiasm, and how alive she felt with him. The contrast between the two experiences was striking, each appealing to different parts of her soul. One offered peace and depth, the other excitement and spontaneity. Mia was caught in the middle, her heart divided.

Finishing her wine, Mia decided that to move forward, she needed more than just reflection; she required clarity. The next day, she would seek advice from someone who had always guided her through her toughest decisions—her older brother, Michael. With his pragmatic outlook and deep understanding of Mia, Michael often had a way of simplifying the complex web of human emotions.

Mia set her alarm for an early morning, and her plan was clear. She would meet Michael for breakfast at their favorite cafe by the river, where they had shared many significant conversations. As Mia prepared for bed, her thoughts were a mixture of anticipation and apprehension. Tomorrow, she hoped, would bring her a step closer to understanding which path her heart truly wanted to take.

CHAPTER 4

THE ART OF JEALOUSY

The soft hues of dawn draped over the cityscape as Mia found herself sitting by the window of their favorite café, a quaint little spot nestled by the tranquil flow of the river. Across from her sat Michael, her brother, his eyes reflecting the same familial warmth that she found so comforting. The aroma of freshly brewed coffee mingled with the gentle breeze coming in through the open window, setting the perfect ambiance for their heartfelt conversation.

"Mia, you seem distant this morning. What's on your mind?" Michael asked, his concern evident in his voice as he sipped his espresso.

Mia sighed, her gaze drifting momentarily towards the rippling waters outside. "It's Alex and Jamie," she confessed, her voice tinged with uncertainty. "I just... I don't know how to navigate this situation."

Michael leaned forward; his expression attentive. "Tell me what's been going on."

Mia took a deep breath, gathering her thoughts before she spoke. "Well, you know how Alex and I have been friends. We've always had this undeniable connection, but lately, things have been different. I can't shake off this feeling that there might be something more between us."

Michael nodded understandingly, his eyes reflecting empathy. "And Jamie?"

Mia's lips curved into a rueful smile. "Jamie is... different. We've only known each other for a short while, but there's something about him that draws me in. He's kind, attentive, and he makes me feel special in a way that I haven't felt before."

Silence settled between them as Mia grappled with her emotions, the weight of her indecision palpable in the air. Michael reached out, placing a reassuring hand on hers, offering silent support.

"I know it's complicated, Mia," he said softly. "But maybe it's worth exploring these feelings, both for Alex and Jamie. Sometimes, the heart knows what it wants, even when the mind is unsure."

Mia nodded slowly, a sense of clarity beginning to dawn upon her. "You're right, Michael. Maybe I've been too afraid to confront my feelings, but I owe it to myself to be honest and open about what I want."

As the morning sun cast its golden glow over the river, Mia felt a sense of peace wash over her. She knew that the path ahead wouldn't be easy, but with Michael by her side and the promise of a new day, she felt ready to embrace the journey and follow her heart, wherever it may lead.

Later that night the city was excited as the annual cultural festival kicked off, transforming the streets into a rainbow of colors, sounds, and smells. Stalls lined the avenues, each offering glimpses into different cultures and cuisines, while stages set up at various points hosted performances ranging from folk dances to contemporary music. It was the perfect backdrop for unexpected encounters and heightened emotions.

Mia, clad in a light summer dress that fluttered with the gentle breeze, was caught up in the vibrant energy of the festival. She had planned to meet Clara for an afternoon of cultural immersion, but as fate would have it, Alex had also decided to attend the festival, each without knowing the other's plans.

Alex, an enthusiast for vibrant gatherings, found Mia first. His approach was marked by a flamboyant wave and a wide grin. "Mia! What a fantastic surprise!" he exclaimed, sweeping her into a brief, exuberant hug that lifted her feet off the ground. His energy was infectious, and within moments, he was guiding her toward a stage where a band was setting up, promising her the best live music the city had to offer.

Mia couldn't help but be swept up in Alex's enthusiasm as they made their way through the crowd. His passion for life was palpable, each word and gesture brimming with excitement. They danced near the stage, the rhythm of the drums syncing with their hearts beating. Alex's eyes sparkled with mischief and delight as he twirled her around, drawing more than a few admiring glances from onlookers.

However, the light-hearted atmosphere shifted when Jamie entered the scene. His approach was quieter, more reserved, but no less impactful. Spotting

Mia in the crowd, his expression was a complex mix of joy and a hint of displeasure at seeing her so close to Alex.

"Hello, Mia," Jamie said, his voice calm but carrying an undercurrent of tension. "It seems we've all had the same idea today." His gaze flickered between Mia and Alex, a polite smile not quite reaching his eyes.

Mia felt a tug in her chest, the joy of the festival now tinged with a hint of conflict. She introduced them, slightly strained, "Alex, this is Jamie. Jamie, Alex." The men shook hands, their smiles tight, the grip perhaps a tad firmer than necessary.

As the afternoon progressed, a coincidental meeting became a silent battle for her attention. With his flair for the dramatic, Alex lavished Mia with compliments and laughter, often pulling her into the dance or trying exotic food from one of the stalls. Each act seemed designed to impress, to stake his claim.

On the other hand, Jamie used his profound knowledge of art and culture to sway Mia. He guided her through an exhibition of local artists displayed at the festival, discussing the techniques and stories behind each piece with an enlightening and intimate depth. His comments were thoughtful and intended to resonate with Mia's artistic sensibilities.

Mia felt increasingly overwhelmed by Alex's bold charisma and Jamie's subtle intellect. Once a playground of cultural delights, the festival now felt like an arena. She appreciated both men's efforts, yet their competition's intensity left her fatigued. It was flattering yet exhausting to be the focus of such a competition. Mia excused herself to find Clara, needing a moment to escape and gather her thoughts. Clara, upon hearing the developments, offered a wry smile. "Sounds like you're in quite a predicament, my friend. Both seem eager to win you over, but at what cost?" Her question lingered in the air, as moving as the music drifted from the nearby stage.

Mia sighed, watching the festivalgoers moving around in high spirits. "I know they mean well, but this rivalry... it's making things complicated."

Clara nodded; her eyes sympathetic. "Maybe it's time they heard that from you, Mia. Clear the air before it suffocates you."

Mia knew Clara was right. As night fell and the festival lights twinkled like stars to come to earth, she resolved to speak to both Alex and Jamie. Tomorrow, she decided, would be the day she addressed the growing tension, hoping to restore peace and clarity to what had become an emotional whirlwind.

Rejuvenated by the crisp night air, Mia walked slowly away from the bustling festival, her mind racing about the events. The cheerful noise of the celebration receded behind her, replaced by the quiet of the city's more tranquil streets. This quieter environment allowed her to reflect more deeply on her situation.

Mia pondered the complexity of her feelings towards Alex and Jamie. Alex, with his unbridled enthusiasm and zest for life, made her feel alive in an exhilarating way. His presence was like a bright flame—vivid and warm. On the other hand, Jamie's intellectual depth and calm demeanor offered her a different kind of warmth, more like a steady glow from embers, comforting and enlightening. Both men appealed to other parts of her soul, each enriching yet complicating her life with their affections.

With this resolution firm in her mind, Mia reached her apartment. The building was quiet, and most of the residents were likely still enjoying the festival's final delights. Once inside, she made herself a cup of herbal tea, the soothing aroma helping to calm her further. She settled onto her small balcony; the city lights a faint echo of the festival's vibrancy.

Mia drafted the words she would say to Alex and Jamie as she sipped her tea. It was crucial to communicate her thoughts clearly and sincerely to maintain the respect and friendship she cherished with both. She wrote down key points, ensuring her message was balanced and fair, emphasizing her respect for them and her desire to enjoy their company without the undercurrent of competition.

Thinking ahead, Mia considered the possible outcomes of her discussions. She hoped for understanding but braced herself for any resistance they might show. These conversations could change the dynamics of her relationships with them for better or worse. The thought was daunting, but Mia felt empowered by her decision to steer the course of her emotional journey.

After her tea was finished, Mia prepared for bed. Her thoughts slowly settled into a plan of action for the next day. She knew honest conversations were the foundation of any strong relationship and was ready to lay down those stones.

As she drifted off to sleep, Mia felt a mixture of nerves and relief. The day's challenges had been many, but they had crystallized her resolve to address the situation head-on. Tomorrow's conversations would be pivotal, but she felt ready to face them with a clear mind and a steady heart.

Mia awoke the next morning to the gentle caress of sunlight filtering through her curtains, casting soft patterns across her room. Despite the turmoil of the previous day's events, she felt a profound sense of purpose. Today was the day she would seek to balance the scales between her flourishing relationships with Alex and Jamie, striving for honesty and clarity in her interactions.

After a quiet breakfast, Mia sat at her kitchen table, reviewing the notes she had made the night before. Each word was weighed with care, crafted to convey her feelings without causing unnecessary hurt. She appreciated Alex and Jamie deeply, and her priority was to preserve the unique relationships she had fostered with them, even as she addressed the competition that had begun to strain those bonds.

First, she called Alex, arranging to meet him for coffee in the late morning at a quaint café known for its secluded garden. It was a spot where they could talk openly, away from the crowded, vibrant settings where they usually met. As she prepared to leave, Mia chose her outfit with deliberation, opting for something casual yet composed, reflecting her mood and the serious nature of their conversation.

Upon arriving at the café, Mia found Alex already there, his usually bright demeanor somewhat subdued. The initial greetings were cordial, and as they ordered their coffee, the casual small talk was tinged with an undercurrent of anticipation. Once seated in a quiet corner of the garden, with blossoming flowers all around and the soft sound of a water feature, Mia took a deep breath and began.

"Alex, I've enjoyed the energy and excitement you bring into my life," Mia started, her voice steady. "Our adventures are something I truly cherish. However, I feel it's important to address the competitive tension that's been developing between you and Jamie. It's putting a strain on me, and I value our friendship too much to let it become a source of stress."

Alex listened intently, his expression a mixture of concern and understanding. He nodded slowly, taking a moment to formulate his response. "Mia, I never intended to make you feel pressured. I guess my competitive side and my growing feelings for you got the better of me. I'm sorry if it caused you any discomfort."

Mia appreciated his openness and willingness to understand. They continued to discuss their feelings and expectations, ensuring that rivalry would not overshadow their friendship. By the end of their conversation, a new understanding had been reached. It promised to respect Mia's feelings and preserve the spontaneity and joy of their connection without the competitive edge.

Feeling relieved and hopeful, Mia left the café to meet Jamie in the afternoon at a local art gallery. The morning's successful conversation had bolstered her confidence, and she was ready to navigate the more reflective and possibly deeper waters of her relationship with Jamie.

Mia reflected on the morning's events as she walked to the gallery. The conversation with Alex had gone better than she had hoped, and she felt a lightness in her step. She was determined to bring the same level of clarity and honesty to her meeting with Jamie, hopeful that he, too, would understand and respect her feelings.

CHAPTER 5

DUAL INVITATIONS

The morning sun cast a gentle glow through the curtains of Mia's apartment as she sat sipping her coffee, the steam swirling upwards in lazy spirals. Today promised an eventful day, as Jamie had invited her to the same prestigious art gala that Alex was supposed to attend. This annual event celebrated emerging and established artists alike.

As she prepared for the evening, Mia chose her outfit carefully—a sleek, midnight blue gown that flowed gracefully to her ankles and a delicate silver necklace that caught the light with every movement. Her attire was a statement and armor, readying her for the night ahead.

Upon arriving at the gala, the venue's grandeur struck her immediately. The high ceilings were adorned with intricate murals, and crystal chandeliers cast a sparkling light over the guests. Sculptures and paintings filled the space, each a testament to the vibrant creativity of the city's artists.

Alex was the first to greet her, his presence as dynamic as the abstract art on display. Dressed sharply in a tailored suit, he exuded a charm that was hard to ignore. With a flourish, he offered Mia a glass of champagne, his smile infectious.

"Mia, you look stunning," Alex complimented, his eyes appreciating her effort. There's a sculptor here whose work I think you'll find truly revolutionary."

Alex's enthusiasm for the art was palpable as they walked through the gallery. He discussed the pieces with impressive knowledge, his explanations adding depth to the visual feast before them. However, Mia could sense Alex's underlying intent—to dazzle her with his charm and insight, making the evening as much about their interaction as the art itself.

It wasn't long before Jamie found them. His approach was more reserved than Alex's exuberance but no less compelling. Jamie's attire was elegant, starkly contrasting Alex's flamboyant style. His greeting was warm, though his demeanor was slightly stiff, likely due to seeing Mia with Alex.

"Good evening, Mia. You're a vision tonight," Jamie said, his compliment more measured but sincere. "There's a series of paintings here that encapsulate the essence of the Romantic period. Would you care to see them?"

Torn between two compelling offers, Mia decided to spend time with Alex and Jamie throughout the evening. As the night progressed, it became clear that the gala was not just a showcase of art but also a backdrop for their ongoing rivalry.

As the music wound down and the applause echoed through the grand hall, Mia felt the weight of the evening's events. Alex and Jamie were exceptional in their ways, but the rivalry was becoming increasingly burdensome.

Retreating to a quieter part of the gallery, Mia found a secluded spot near a small, beautifully lit water fountain. The sound of the water was soothing, a gentle reminder of the world beyond the gala's competitive atmosphere.

In the tranquility of this hidden corner, Mia reflected on her feelings. The night had been a whirlwind of art, rivalry, charm, and challenge. She realized that while both men had impressive qualities, their ongoing competition needed to be more consistent with the genuine connections she sought.

As the gala neared its end, Mia knew that a decision loomed. She needed to address the situation and clarify her need for authenticity and depth in her relationships with them.

Mia stepped out of the grandiose venue into the refreshing coolness of the night, her mind a swirl of conflicting emotions and half-formed decisions. She strolled down the cobblestone path that led away from the gala's laughter and light, allowing the city's serene silence at night to calm her tumultuous thoughts.

With each step, the din of the event faded, replaced by the soft rustle of leaves and the distant hum of late-night city life. The contrast between the gala's intense energy and the streets' peaceful solitude provided Mia with a necessary perspective. She needed to recalibrate and align her next actions with the insights she had gained from tonight's experiences.

Mia contemplated the interactions of the evening—the way Alex and Jamie had each vied for her attention. Both had shown qualities she admired: Alex, with his vivacious passion for art and life, and Jamie, with his thoughtful insights and calm demeanor.

When she reached her apartment, the familiar surroundings welcomed her with open arms. Inside, she quickly jotted down her thoughts and the key points she wanted to discuss with Alex and Jamie. Clarity was crucial, not only to convey her feelings effectively but also to maintain the integrity of each relationship moving forward.

Before retiring to bed, Mia stood at her window, looking over the city that seemed to sleep peacefully below. The stars twinkled above, indifferent spectators to human complexities. Mia felt a wave of resolve wash over her. She was ready to face the challenges ahead, to steer her relationships into waters free of rivalry and misunderstandings.

Resting her head on her pillow that night, Mia felt more prepared. Tomorrow, she would set the stage for honest conversations, hoping to foster a deeper understanding and respect among them. She drifted off to sleep with a sense of purpose, knowing that while the path ahead was uncertain, her intentions were clear and guided by sincerity and respect for Alex and Jamie.

Mia woke early the next morning, the first rays of dawn casting a gentle light that filled her room with a soft, golden hue. She lay in bed for a moment, allowing the peacefulness of the morning to seep into her being, fortifying her resolve for the conversations ahead. Today, she would begin the delicate process of untangling the complicated web of emotions and rivalries that had formed around her.

After a quiet breakfast, Mia reflected, revisiting the notes she had made the night before. She refined her thoughts, precisely choosing her words, aiming to convey her feelings without giving rise to defensiveness or conflict. Her approach needed to be firm yet empathetic, a balance that would allow her to maintain the integrity of each friendship.

By mid-morning, Mia was ready. She left her apartment feeling a mixture of nervous anticipation and determined calm. She had arranged to meet Jamie. The vibrant café they were meeting at was buzzing with the lively energy of the city's morning rush. The aroma of coffee and the clatter of dishes provided a backdrop that, she hoped, would help keep the meeting informal and grounded.

Mia repeated her earlier approach, expressing her appreciation for Jamie's thoughtful presence and desire for a less competitive, more genuine interaction. Jamie, ever the introspective, listened intently, nodding in understanding as Mia spoke.

Their conversation delved deeper into their expectations and how they could better support one another as potential romantic interests and as friends. Jamie appreciated Mia's honesty, and they parted with a mutual understanding that strengthened their bond.

Returning home, Mia felt a weight lift from her shoulders. The conversations had gone as well as she had hoped, and a path forward was now clear. She knew that maintaining these newly set boundaries would require constant communication and respect, but she was ready to handle it.

As she sat down that evening to write down her reflections on the day, Mia felt a profound sense of accomplishment. She had navigated a challenging situation with grace and emerged stronger.

CHAPTER 6

UNDER THE STARS

As dusk embraced the city, turning the horizon Into a rich tapestry of purples and blues, Mia went to the rooftop where Jamie had arranged their dinner. The building was one of the tallest in that part of the city, and its rooftop garden offered a panoramic view that promised a breathtaking backdrop. Her heart fluttered with anticipation and nerves, curious about what the evening held.

Jamie greeted her at the elevator, his smile bright and welcoming. The rooftop was transformed into a private oasis, with soft lanterns casting a gentle glow and a small table set elegantly for two. The city lights twinkled below them, mirroring the stars beginning to pierce the twilight above.

"Jamie, this is beautiful," Mia said, genuinely impressed by the thought and care he had put into creating such a romantic setting.

"I'm glad you like it," Jamie responded, leading her to the table. "I thought a night under the stars might give us a different perspective, a peaceful place to talk and connect."

As they settled into their seats, a waiter quietly served the first course, a delicately prepared appetizer that paired perfectly with the crisp evening air. The conversation began lightly, with both sharing anecdotes from their week, but as the plates were cleared, Jamie's demeanor shifted to something more serious.

"Mia," he began, his voice steady but filled with emotion, "I've been thinking a lot about us, about what I want in the future, and how deeply I care for you." He paused, searching her eyes for a sign of her feelings. "I see a future with you that's not just about shared interests or momentary passions but a deep, enduring partnership."

Mia listened, moved by his words. Jamie's sincerity in voice and openness in expression were disarming. He spoke of stability, emotional support, and building a life together that would weather any storm.

"I know life is unpredictable," Jamie continued, "but whatever happens, I want you to know I'm here for you. I believe in us, in the strength of what we're building together." His hand reached across the table, fingers gently brushing hers.

Mia felt a warmth spread through her, touched by his commitment and clarity. It was a contrast to the passionate, often tumultuous interactions with Alex. Here with Jamie, under the blanket of night, she felt a peace she had longed for.

As the main course arrived, their conversation deepened. Jamie shared his thoughts on relationships and the importance of trust, mutual respect, and support. He talked about his past and the lessons learned from relationships that taught him what truly mattered.

Mia shared her thoughts, expressing her desire for a relationship that felt like a safe harbor and a place of mutual growth and understanding. "Jamie, hearing you speak about the future like this is exciting and overwhelming," she admitted. "But it's also exactly what I've been hoping for—stability with someone who truly understands and supports me."

The meal continued under the stars, each course enhancing the depth of their connection. The city below them buzzed with life, yet time seemed to slow on the rooftop, allowing them to savor the moment fully.

Jamie took a deep breath as they moved on to dessert, a rich chocolate fondue that mirrored the sweetness of the evening. "Mia, this is just one evening, but I hope it can be a foundation for many more. I want to build something lasting with you, something real."

Mia's heart felt full as she processed his words. The promise of a stable, supportive future was alluring, especially given her recent tumultuous experiences. "Jamie, tonight has been incredible. Your honesty and beautiful setting are rarer than I could have asked for. I need time to think about all this, but please know I am just as committed to exploring where this path might lead us."

As the evening drew close, they stood together at the rooftop's edge, looking out over the city. The stars above them witnessed their growing connection, promising potential and hope.

Jamie escorted her back to the elevator, their goodbye lingering, a promise of more. Mia left the building feeling a mixture of contentment and contemplation, her thoughts as vast as the night sky above.

The gentle night breeze accompanied Mia as she strolled through the quiet streets, her mind dancing between the serene joy of the evening and the deeper reflections it provoked. Jamie's declaration, offered beneath a celestial tapestry, resonated with a part of her that craved the tranquility he embodied. Yet, she could not shake the vibrant allure of her connection with Alex, marked by its fervent spontaneity.

As Mia approached her apartment building, the contrasting emotions tugged at her heart with equal fervor. She realized that her journey wasn't just about choosing between two men—it was a deeper quest to reconcile the disparate parts of her desires: the thrill of unpredictability versus the comfort of stability.

Upon entering her apartment, Mia slipped off her shoes and padded to her small balcony, again drawn to the cityscape that sprawled under the starlit sky. The world seemed to hold its breath, and Mia felt a rare sense of clarity in that stillness. This evening with Jamie illuminated an undeniably appealing path, yet she understood that her heart was not yet ready to commit to a single course.

Retrieving her journal from the living room, Mia poured her swirling thoughts onto paper, which always helped her navigate her emotions. She wrote about the evening—the intimacy of the conversation, the thoughtful ambiance Jamie had created, and the earnestness of his feelings. She noted her reactions, how each word from Jamie had made her feel seen and valued, yet how she also yearned for the sparks of excitement that came with her interactions with Alex.

Mia's writing gradually shifted from recounting the evening to exploring her feelings about stability and excitement. She questioned whether the depth of connection she felt with Jamie could sustain her or whether the absence of thrill, the kind Alex provided, would leave her wanting.

The clock ticked past midnight as Mia continued to write. Her words began to form a map of her emotional landscape, revealing valleys of doubt and peaks of realization. It became clear that her decision would influence her romantic life and define her understanding of love and partnership.

Eventually, Mia closed her journal, her mind saturated with thought yet oddly at peace. She understood that while tonight had not brought a definitive answer, it had sharpened her understanding of what she truly valued and what she needed to further explore.

Mia prepared for bed, her thoughts slowly settling like dust after a storm.

CHAPTER 7

THE ADVENTURE

The city at night held a different kind of magic, transforming familiar streets into a canvas of shadows and lights, ripe for exploration and discovery. Alex invited Mia into this nocturnal wonderland, promising an adventure that would capture her imagination and perhaps sway her heart.

Mia met Alex at the agreed location, a little-known entry point to the city's abandoned subway tunnels—an urban explorer's dream. The air was crisp, carrying the faintest chill of the coming night as the last streaks of sunset faded into twilight. Alex, equipped with a backpack filled with photography gear and safety supplies, greeted her with an infectious enthusiasm that immediately lifted her spirits.

"Ready for an adventure?" Alex asked, his eyes twinkling with excitement. Mia nodded, feeling a surge of adrenaline at the prospect of what lay ahead. Alex's element was the thrill of discovery, the allure of the unknown, and he was eager to share it with her.

As they descended into the depths of the old subway system, the sounds of the city muffled by layers of earth and concrete, Mia felt like they were stepping into another world. The tunnels, lit only by the beams of their flashlights, stretched endlessly before them, their walls echoing back the soft sounds of their movements.

Alex confidently led the way, his familiarity with the terrain evident in his sure steps and occasional pauses to point out interesting graffiti or architectural features. Mia's initial apprehension gave way to fascination as she began to see the beauty in the decay: the way the light played off the moisture-laden walls, the patterns of rust and peeling paint that told stories of years gone by.

After navigating several twists and turns, they arrived at a tunnel section that opened into a vast underground chamber. Here, Alex set up his tripod, aiming his camera at a particularly striking view where the tunnel curved sharply, creating a dramatic interplay of light and shadow.

"The way the urban landscape can be so unexpectedly beautiful—it's what I love about photography," Alex explained as he adjusted his camera settings. "Capturing these moments, it's like freezing a piece of hidden history in time."

Mia watched him work, seeing the passion and care he put into each shot. She took out her camera, a recent gift from Alex, and began experimenting with angles and settings, encouraged by his tips and the supportive glances he shot her way.

As they worked side by side, the thrill of the adventure grew. Exploring and capturing the forgotten parts of the city was exhilarating, and Mia found herself caught up in Alex's excitement. It reminded her of what had drawn her to him in the first place: his zest for life, his refusal to simply walk the beaten path, and his ability to find wonder in the overlooked.

Hours slipped by as they explored further, taking photographs, and sharing stories. When they finally decided to head back, their path illuminated by the soft glow of their flashlights, Mia felt a renewed appreciation for Alex's spontaneous side, which complemented her more structured nature.

Emerging from the subway entrance, the night sky greeted them with the brilliance of countless stars. The city had transformed once again into a quiet, peaceful landscape under the celestial canopy. Alex stopped, turning to Mia with a hopeful look.

"Tonight was about sharing my world with you, Mia," he said earnestly. "I hope it reminded you of our good times and adventures, which are still waiting for us."

Mia reached for his hand, gently squeezing it. "It did, Alex," she admitted, her voice soft but clear in the night air. "Tonight was special. These moments remind me of how much fun we have together."

As they returned to the city center, Mia's mind was alive with thoughts. The adventure had indeed rekindled her excitement for the spontaneity Alex brought into her life. Yet, she knew her decision could not be swayed by a single night, no matter how magical. The complexities of her feelings for Alex and Jamie required more than an exciting adventure to untangle.

Mia continued her solitary walk home, each step echoing on the pavement as she navigated the city's sleeping streets. Her adventure with Alex that night had filled her with anticipation and reflection. Even while Mia could not help but be enthralled with the excitement of their urban tour, she realized that these kinds of experiences constituted but a small portion of the complex puzzle of a relationship.

As she walked, her thoughts turned to Jamie, the contrasting nature of her connections with him and Alex becoming ever more apparent. Where Alex sparked a vibrant flame of excitement and unpredictability, Jamie offered a gentle glow of stability and depth. This difference was fascinating and challenging, and Mia found herself wrestling with the implications for her heart and future.

Mia reflected on what she truly sought in a partner as the city's familiar landmarks guided her steps. Was it the constant surge of adrenaline that Alex provided or the comforting harbor of understanding that Jamie offered? Or perhaps, she mused, it was a balance of both worlds—a synthesis of excitement and security that she yearned for.

Reaching her apartment building, Mia paused at the entrance, taking a moment to look up at the star-filled sky. The vastness above seemed to mirror the breadth of her internal landscape—filled with questions, possibilities, and a quiet hope.

Once inside her apartment, Mia didn't head straight to bed. Instead, she felt compelled to capture the night's experiences and her swirling thoughts in her journal. Settling at her small writing desk, she opened her journal to a new page and began to write. With each word, she traced the contours of her evening with Alex, the thrill of discovery, and the deeper reflections it provoked about her romantic journey.

Mia wrote about the sharp contrast between the evening's adventure and Jamie's serene dinners and conversations. She pondered how each man brought out different aspects of her personality and how each relationship nourished her uniquely. Her pen moved fluidly as if guided by a newfound clarity that the night's adventures had unlocked.

As she continued to write, Mia considered the importance of aligning her choices with her core values and desires. The allure of adventure with Alex was undeniable, but she also craved the emotional depth and understanding that Jamie brought into her life. The decision she faced was not just about choosing between two men but honoring her heart's complexities.

In the tranquil silence of her room, with only the soft hum of the city as her lullaby, Mia felt a reassuring sense of peace envelop her. The evening's adventures and her introspective journaling allowed her to approach her tangled emotions with a new level of clarity and perspective. As she drifted toward sleep, her thoughts began to quiet, and a gentle readiness for the future settled in her heart.

The next morning, Mia awoke to the gentle rays of sunlight filtering through her curtains, casting a warm glow that filled her room with a soft, inviting light. Refreshed and invigorated by a night of deep, restful sleep, she felt more equipped to continue her journey of emotional discovery. Today was not about thrilling adventures or deep conversations under the stars; it was about reflection and personal understanding.

As she lay in bed for a few moments, Mia planned her day with intention. She spent the morning in solitude, visiting the city's botanical garden. In this place, she could be surrounded by nature and find a quiet space to reflect on her relationships with Alex and Jamie. The serene environment would provide the perfect backdrop for her thoughts, allowing her to further explore her feelings without the immediate pressures of decision-making.

Mia's morning in the botanical garden would be a time for solitude, but the afternoon promised another layer of engagement. She planned to meet with Clara, her ever-supportive friend, to discuss her recent realizations and seek advice on navigating the emotional complexities she faced. Clara's insights have always helped Mia to see her situation from new perspectives, and Mia looked forward to gaining more wisdom from their conversation.

Determined to make the most out of the day, Mia got out of bed and began her morning routine. She felt a hopeful anticipation for the insights the day might bring, and she was ready to face whatever emotions and decisions lay ahead with courage and openness.

Mia stepped out of her apartment; her spirit buoyed by a sense of purpose. She was seeking answers and embracing the journey itself, with all its twists and turns. As she walked toward the botanical garden, her heart was open to the lessons of love and life she was continually learning, each step a testament to her growth and resilience.

CHAPTER 8

DECISION'S EVE

Mia and Clara's path was a patchwork of light and shadow as the late afternoon sunlight seeped through the old oak trees' leaves in the city park. Mia had always found this park a comforting place, a green sanctuary amid the city's ceaseless energy. Today, she needed that comfort more than ever as she grappled with a decision that felt increasingly monumental.

Clara, ever perceptive, noticed the slight furrow in Mia's brow as they found a quiet bench by the pond. "You look like you're carrying the world on your shoulders," she said gently, giving Mia an encouraging smile. "Talk to me."

Mia sighed, her eyes tracing the pond's tranquil waters before meeting Clara's steady gaze. "It's about Alex and Jamie," Mia began, her voice tinged with uncertainty. "I'm at a crossroads, and each path leads me in different directions. Alex makes life exciting and unpredictable with his boundless energy and thirst for adventure. But Jamie, with his thoughtful nature and intellectual depth, offers a kind of stability and understanding that I deeply value."

Clara nodded, her expression thoughtful. "It sounds like you're torn between a whirlwind and a harbor. Both are essential in their way. But which do you feel you need more at this stage of your life?"

The question lingered, prompting Mia to delve deeper into her feelings. "I love the excitement Alex brings into my life; it's invigorating. But sometimes, it feels overwhelming, as if I'm constantly trying to catch my breath," Mia confessed. "With Jamie, it's different. His presence is calming, and our conversations are so enriching. I feel grounded and understood."

"As wonderful as both sounds, it's important to consider not just the moments of excitement or calm but how each relationship aligns with your long-term goals and values," Clara advised. She reached into her bag, pulling out a notepad and pen. "Let's try something. Let's list the pros and cons of each relationship. It might help you visualize your thoughts more clearly."

Together, they began to list the attributes of each relationship. For Alex, the pros were his adventurous spirit, his ability to challenge Mia to step out of her comfort zone, and the intense chemistry they shared. The cons, however, included the lack of stability and the emotional highs and lows that sometimes left Mia feeling drained.

For Jamie, the pros included his intellectual compatibility with Mia, the emotional security he provided, and the mutual respect that defined their interactions. The cons were fewer but significant; Mia sometimes missed the spark of spontaneity that Alex brought to her life.

As they reviewed the lists, Clara asked, "Which qualities do you see as essential for your happiness and growth in the long run? And can you accept the trade-offs that come with each choice?"

Mia pondered the question, her gaze drifting to a couple laughing across the pond. She realized that while she cherished the excitement Alex brought into her life, she yearned for more deeply the sense of partnership and understanding she found with Jamie. The thrill of adventure was exhilarating, but the day-to-day reality of shared values and mutual support aligns more closely with her vision for the future.

"Clara, I think I'm leaning towards Jamie," Mia admitted, a sense of relief washing over her as she spoke aloud. "The stability and intellectual connection we have... it feels right. It feels like what I need to thrive, not just survive."

Clara smiled warmly, squeezing Mia's hand. "It sounds like your heart has been speaking to you. Sometimes, we just need a little help listening to it."

Mia felt like a weight had been lifted off her shoulders as the sun started to fall, covering the park in a golden glow. The decision was not yet final, and there were still conversations with Alex and Jamie, but Mia felt more confident in her path forward.

Mia walked home from the park with a lighter step, each movement reflecting her newly found resolve. The setting sun painted the clouds in hues of orange and purple, mirroring the sense of peace and clarity that had settled over her after her conversation with Clara. Her mind, often a battleground of competing desires and fears, now harbored a quiet confidence in the decision she leaned towards making.

Arriving at her apartment, Mia didn't head straight indoors. Instead, she lingered on the sidewalk, looking up at the expanse of the evening sky that stretched above her urban neighborhood. The first stars were beginning to twinkle, and the crescent moon hung like a silver boat on the darkening sea of dusk. In these quiet moments, she found that the magnitude of her life's choices felt most profound yet bearable.

Once inside, Mia didn't surrender to the usual fatigue that followed an emotionally charged day. Instead, she felt energized, compelled to organize her thoughts and prepare for the conversations that awaited her with Alex and Jamie. She opened her little, well-used writing desk, took out a blank sheet of paper, and started to write down her ideas. She outlined what she appreciated about each relationship, her concerns, and how she envisioned her future with Jamie, the man who seemed to offer what she most needed at this juncture in her life.

Writing down her thoughts helped solidify her resolve. It was an affirmation exercise, a way to remind herself of the reasons behind her learning and to prepare herself to communicate these reasons clearly and compassionately. Mia knew that while her heart had spoken, verbalizing her decision to Alex and Jamie required a different kind of courage.

With her notes prepared, Mia moved to the kitchen to make herself a light dinner. Cooking was another form of meditation for her, a way to ground herself in the present and focus on the simple, tactile task of preparing food. As she chopped vegetables and heated the pan, her mind rehearsed the upcoming dialogues, imagining different responses and preparing herself for the emotional complexities they would entail.

Dinner was a quiet affair, eaten at her small dining table with the soft hum of city life as her background music. After clearing up, Mia decided to take a brief walk around her neighborhood. The night was mild, and the streets were quiet, save for the occasional passerby or the distant sound of traffic. Walking helped her digest her meal and thoughts, allowing her to step back and view her impending decision from different angles.

As she walked, Mia reflected on the growth she had experienced over the past weeks. Each conversation with Alex and Jamie and every introspective moment she shared with Clara contributed to a deeper understanding of herself and her needs in a relationship. It was clear now that her path forward with Jamie was not just a choice made by comparing pros and cons, but a decision deeply rooted in her personal growth and search for a fulfilling partnership.

Returning to her apartment, Mia felt ready. Tomorrow, she will first meet with Alex to share her decision. She knew it would be a difficult conversation, but one she was prepared to handle with honesty and empathy. Her heart felt calm, her thoughts clear as she readied herself for bed.

As Mia settled into bed, the gentle hum of the city seemed to echo her inner calm. She had traversed the complexities of her emotions, and now, with her decision made, she felt an anchoring sense of purpose. Her thoughts drifted towards tomorrow, to the conversations that awaited her, each imbued with the potential to reshape her life's trajectory.

Lying in the quiet of her room, Mia rehearsed what she would say to Alex. She envisioned herself speaking with grace and sincerity, expressing her gratitude for the joy and vibrancy he had brought into her life while conveying her need to pursue the stability and intellectual connection Jamie offered. She practiced her words, wanting to ensure that her gratitude and respect for Alex were evident despite the painful nature of the conversation.

Mia knew that the morning would come soon enough, bringing with it the reality of her choices. She planned to meet Alex at their favorite park, which had memories of laughter and deep conversations, hoping the familiar, peaceful setting would provide a gentle backdrop for their talk.

As she drifted off to sleep, Mia felt a mix of anticipation and sorrow. While confident in her decision, hurting Alex weighed heavily on her. Yet, she understood that honesty was the kindest gift she could offer herself and him.

Mia's room bathed in the soft silver light of the moon, her breathing deep even as she slept. Tomorrow's challenges loomed, but for tonight, she found solace in the clarity of her decision and the quiet support of the night around her.

CHAPTER 9

CHOOSING PATHS

The morning brought a gentle radiance that filled Mia's apartment with a soft, inviting light. It was a new day, ripe with the promise of beginnings and resolutions. Mia had spent a restless night, her thoughts a whirlwind of emotions and scenarios, but as dawn broke, so did her resolve to solidify. Today, she would make her choice, the decision that would align her heart with her deepest values and aspirations.

After a quiet breakfast, Mia sat at her small kitchen table, a cup of steaming coffee in hand, reflecting on her journey thus far. Alex and Jamie had brought significant joy and lessons into her life, each touching her heart profoundly. Alex, with his adventurous spirit, had shown her the thrill of spontaneity and the beauty of seizing the moment. With his intellectual depth, Jamie had provided her with a sense of peace and a partnership rooted in mutual respect and understanding.

However, recent weeks of reflection and heart-to-heart discussions had made it increasingly clear who truly aligned with her envisioned future. Jamie's steadfast nature and emotional maturity resonated more deeply with her personal goals and the tranquil life she yearned for.

With her decision clear, Mia arranged to meet with Alex in the park and later in the afternoon with Jamie at their favorite café by the river. This place had become a sanctuary of significant conversations and gentle memories. The walk there was calming, each step a steady beat towards a future she chose with intention.

Mia and Alex strolled side by side along the tree-lined path in the park, the gentle rustle of leaves and the distant chirping of birds creating a serene backdrop to their conversation. Mia's heart raced with nervous anticipation as she prepared to broach the topic that had been weighing heavily on her mind.

"Alex," Mia began, her voice soft but resolute, "there's something important I need to talk to you about."

Alex glanced over at her, his expression curious yet attentive. "Sure, Mia. What's on your mind?"

Mia took a deep breath, gathering her thoughts before continuing. "It's about Jamie... and us."

Alex's brow furrowed in confusion. "Jamie? What does Jamie have to do with us?"

Mia hesitated, her words catching in her throat. "I've realized that my feelings for Jamie run deeper than I initially thought. And... I've decided to pursue a relationship with him."

The words hung in the air between them, heavy with the weight of Mia's confession. Alex stopped walking, his eyes searching hers for any sign that she was joking. But the earnestness in Mia's gaze told him otherwise.

"You're choosing Jamie over me?" Alex asked, his voice barely above a whisper.

Mia nodded, her heart aching at the hurt in Alex's eyes. "I know this comes as a shock, Alex. And I'm truly sorry for any pain I've caused you. But I can't deny how I feel any longer."

Alex took a step back, his shoulders slumping in defeat. "I thought... I thought we had something special, Mia. I thought you felt the same way about me."

Mia reached out to gently touch his arm, her voice filled with remorse. "Alex, you mean the world to me. And I'll always cherish the bond we share. But my heart belongs to Jamie, and I can't ignore that any longer."

Tears welled in Alex's eyes as he struggled to process Mia's words. "I don't know if I can accept this, Mia. It feels like... like you're tearing my heart in two."

Mia's own eyes brimmed with tears as she fought to hold back her emotions. "I understand if you need time to come to terms with this, Alex. But please know that I'll always value our friendship, no matter what."

With a heavy heart, Mia turned to continue walking, leaving Alex standing alone on the path, his world shattered by her revelation. As she walked away, Mia couldn't shake the feeling of guilt that gnawed at her insides. But deep down, she knew that she had to follow her heart, even if it meant breaking Alex's in the process.

Jamie was already waiting when Mia arrived, his presence a calm pillar against the gentle morning bustle of the café. His eyes lit up when he saw her, and in that gaze, Mia found the confirmation she needed—that here, in this man, lay a depth of connection and potential for growth that she could no longer deny.

"Mia, you look like you've come to a decision," Jamie said gently, an understanding smile touching his lips as she sat across from him.

"Yes, Jamie, I have," Mia began, her voice steady but filled with emotion. "These past weeks have been a journey for both of us, and you've shown me the depth of your care and the strength of a quiet, steady love. It's something I've come to realize I value deeply, more than I even knew."

Jamie reached across the table, taking her hands in his. "I hope that means what I think it does," he said, his voice hopeful.

Mia nodded, a gentle smile spreading across her face. "It does, Jamie. I choose you and the life we can build together. I believe in us, in the quiet strength of our bond."

The conversation that followed was filled with relief and budding excitement as they began to plan a symbolic event to celebrate their commitment. They decided on a small, intimate gathering at the botanical gardens, which reflected the growth and beauty they found in each other. It would affirm their journey together, surrounded by close friends and family, under the canopy of nature that perfectly mirrored their relationship.

As they left the café, hand in hand, the world around them seemed to echo their joy. The river beside them sparkled under the sun, a path of light that mirrored their path forward.

Mia and Jamie walk along the riverbank, their steps light, their hearts full. They discuss plans for their celebration, each detailing a stitch in the fabric of their future together. Mia feels a profound peace settle over her, the peace of knowing she has chosen a partner who loves her deeply and shares her vision of a life marked by respect, understanding, and quiet joy.

As they paused to watch a pair of ducks glide across the water, Mia knew with unwavering certainty that her decision was right. Her path with Jamie was just beginning, and she walked with eager anticipation and open-hearted commitment.

As Mia and Jamie continued their stroll by the river, the tranquility of the environment deepened their sense of connection. Every shared glance and touch between them echoed the commitment they had just embraced. With the decision, a new layer of intimacy unfurled between them, characterized by a profound understanding and a shared vision for the future.

The air around them was filled with the fresh scent of spring, the trees lining the riverbank awash with the first buds of the season. This renewal in nature mirrored their new beginning, offering a perfect metaphor for the growth and blossoming of their relationship. They discussed the details of their upcoming celebration, each suggestion and decision weaving together into a tapestry of shared dreams.

"We should have some live music," Jamie suggested, enthusiasm lighting up his features. "Something soft and acoustic that blends with the natural setting."

Mia nodded in agreement, her mind already picturing the scene. "And let's use local flowers for the decorations," she added, picturing the vibrant colors and textures that would enhance the beauty of the botanical gardens. "It would be wonderful to have a setting that reflects our love for the natural world and our commitment to sustainability."

As they planned, their ideas flowed effortlessly, their mutual respect and admiration for each other's thoughts evident in every exchange. It was clear that their relationship was not just built on love but also on a deep-seated compatibility that made even the simplest planning feel like an extension of their connection.

The sky was painting itself in tones of orange and pink as the afternoon softly transitioned into the early evening. Mia and Jamie decided to end their perfect day with a quiet dinner at a small bistro overlooking the river. The bistro was a cozy, candlelit haven that offered them a private corner to continue their undisturbed conversations.

Over dinner, they talked about more than just their celebration plans. They shared aspirations for their life together, discussing potential travel destinations, career ambitions, and even the quaint idea of one day adopting a pet. Each topic reinforced their compatibility and the ease with which they envisioned a shared future.

"It feels like we're building something special, something enduring," Jamie said, reaching across the table to squeeze Mia's hand.

Mia smiled, her eyes reflecting the soft candlelight. "I've never been sure of anything," she replied, her voice silky yet filled with conviction. "Choosing you, choosing us—it's the rightest decision I've ever made."

As they finished their meal, the bistro's soft music and the gentle murmur of other diners created a warm background symphony. It was the perfect end to a day marked by significant choices and deep affirmations.

Leaving the bistro, Mia and Jamie walked hand in hand back towards Mia's apartment, the city lights beginning to twinkle in the evening dusk. Their conversation was lightened, filled with laughter and playful banter, yet beneath the lightheartedness was a current of deep joy and anticipation for the life they were planning together.

As they reached Mia's apartment building, their final steps were slow. They did not want the night to end. They paused outside, reluctant to part, "Do you want to go to my apartment for a little while?" Mia asked Jamie. "Sure" Jamie responded. Mia stood at the edge of the balcony, the cool night air caressing her skin as she gazed out at the twinkling city lights below. The soft strains of music floated through the air, mingling with the gentle rustle of leaves in the breeze. Jamie approached her from behind, his footsteps silent on the tiled floor. "You look breathtaking," Jamie whispered, his voice sending shivers down Mia's spine as he wrapped his arms around her waist. Mia leaned back into his embrace, her heart racing at his touch. She turned her head to meet his gaze, and in that moment, the world seemed to fade away, leaving only the two of them. Their lips met in a tender kiss, a silent promise of the love that burned between them. Jamie's hands roamed over Mia's body, igniting a fire that threatened to consume them both. With each caress, each whispered endearment, their passion grew, until they were both lost in the depths of desire. With trembling hands, Jamie traced a path down Mia's spine, sending shivers of anticipation coursing through her. She moaned softly as he pulled her closer, their bodies pressed together in a fierce embrace.

"I need you," Jamie breathed against her lips, his voice husky with longing. Mia nodded, her desire matching his as she reached up to pull him closer. Their clothes fell away forgotten, discarded in their haste to be closer, to feel skin against skin.And then, finally, they were one, their bodies moving together in a dance as old as time itself. Each touch, each kiss, fueled the flames of their passion until they were consumed by the fire of their love. At that moment, there was no past, no future, only the exquisite bliss of being together, of knowing that they had found in each other the missing piece of their souls.And as they lay tangled together in the darkness, their hearts beating as one, Mia knew that she had found her home in Jamie's arms.

"Tomorrow?" Jamie asked a hopeful note in his voice.

"Tomorrow," Mia confirmed with a nod, her smile bright. "And all the tomorrows after that."

With a tender kiss goodnight, hearts full and spirits high, secure in the knowledge that together, they were embarking on a beautiful journey—one paved with love, mutual respect, and endless possibilities.

The echo of the door closing behind her reverberated with a sense of finality and a new beginning. She leaned against it momentarily, allowing the day's emotions to wash over her. The excitement of planning a life with Jamie and the relief of having made a decision that aligned so completely with her values and desires filled her with a profound sense of contentment.

In the quiet of her own space, Mia took a few moments to reflect on the journey that had brought her here. It had been a path fraught with confusion and emotional turmoil but also graced with profound clarity and joy. The contrast between her past uncertainties and her current resolve was stark tonight. She felt anchored, her future with Jamie promising companionship and a partnership that resonated with her deepest self.

Turning on a soft lamp, Mia moved to her small desk where she kept her journal—a companion through many restless nights and reflective mornings. She opened it to a new page and began to write. This entry, however, was different. It was not a pouring out of doubts or a weaving through confusion. Instead, it was a celebration of resolution, a record of a decision that seemed so right that it could only lead to happiness.

Mia wrote about the day, about the joy and love she felt planning their celebration at the botanical gardens, and how each decision they made about the event seemed to reflect their mutual respect and shared dreams. She wrote about the peace that filled her now, which came from knowing she had chosen a partner who loved her and who she could love freely and fully, without reservation.

Mia turned off the lamp and moved to her window, where she looked out over the city. The night was serene, and the stars were visible above, a perfect canopy under which to ponder her future. With optimism in her heart and tranquility in her mind, Mia felt prepared to begin a new chapter in her life, one that would be full of love, compassion, and the delight of traveling together.

CHAPTER 10

NEW BEGINNINGS

The morning sun broke over the city with a clarity that heralded the fresh start Mia and Jamie had embarked upon. Their commitment ceremony in the botanical gardens had been nothing short of magical—a celebration of their love and the new life they were starting together. However, the true test of their relationship was waiting just around the corner, a challenge that would demand every ounce of their mutual respect and understanding.

It began with an unexpected call that Mia received one crisp morning, two weeks after their celebration. It was from her sister, Ellen, who lived abroad and seldom reached out due to her intense work commitments. Ellen's voice was strained, her words rushed. "Mia, I hate to drop this on you, but I need your help. It's Mom. She's had a fall, nothing life-threatening, but she's going to need care, and I can't get away from my project here."

Mia felt her heart lurch. Her mother had always been fiercely independent, and the news of her frailty was shocking. "Of course, I'll help, Ellen. I'll sort things out here and head to Mom's as soon as I can," Mia responded, her mind racing through the logistics.

She hung up and immediately sought out Jamie, who was sorting through emails in their small home office. His concentration shifted to concern as he took in Mia's expression. "What's wrong?" he asked.

Mia explained the situation, her voice steady despite the turmoil inside. "I need to go to her, Jamie. It might be for a few weeks. I know this is terrible timing with everything we've just started here..."

Jamie stood and approached her, his expression softening as he took her hands. "Mia, there's no question about it. You need to be with your mom. We'll make it work. Don't worry about us here; I'll handle things on the home front."

His supportive response was a balm to her frayed nerves. Mia felt a wave of gratitude for Jamie's understanding and flexibility. "Thank you, Jamie. I can't tell you how much this means to me," she said, her eyes moist with a mixture of stress and relief.

Within a day, Mia had packed her bags and was on her way to her mother's house in the countryside. The transition from newlywed bliss to caretaking was abrupt, and Mia struggled with her new role's emotional and physical demands. Each day brought new challenges, from managing her mother's medical appointments to handling her physical therapy sessions. The weight of her mother's dependence, coupled with the distance from Jamie, began to wear on her.

However, Jamie's nightly calls were a lifeline. They talked through everything—from how her day went to how he managed their household affairs back in the city. "How was the doctor's appointment today? Did the new medications seem to help?" Jamie would ask, his voice a steady presence in her chaotic days.

One evening, as Mia sat exhausted on the porch of her mother's house, watching the sunset over the fields, she reflected on the strain of the past weeks. In this moment of solitude, she fully realized the depth of the bond she and Jamie shared. Despite the physical distance, their relationship had not just endured; it had deepened. They were learning to navigate life's unexpected storms together, their commitment to each other providing strength and comfort.

Mia decided then that she needed to express her gratitude to Jamie for his unwavering support during this ordeal. Planning a small surprise for him, she arranged for a weekend getaway for both as soon as her mother was stable enough for her to take a short break. It would be their chance to reconnect, to reaffirm their bond away from the pressures of daily life.

Jamie drove out to join her in the countryside when the weekend arrived. The reunion was sweet, filled with laughter and shared stories. They spent their days exploring the local sights and their evenings wrapped up in each other's company, reinforcing the foundation of their relationship.

As they sat together one evening, watching the stars blanket the sky, Mia leaned into Jamie. "These past weeks have shown me just how strong we are together," she said, her voice soft but clear in the quiet night. "I couldn't have gotten through this without you."

Jamie squeezed her hand, his response simple but heartfelt. "We're in this together, Mia. Whatever comes, we'll face it side by side."

As the weekend drew close, Mia and Jamie packed their belongings, their spirits refreshed, and their connection rejuvenated. The drive back to the city was filled with a comfortable silence, each lost in thoughts of gratitude and renewed commitment. The challenges of the past few weeks had been a crucible, tempering their relationship into something stronger, more resilient.

Back in the city, the couple settled into a new routine with an ease that spoke to their deepened understanding of each other. Mia managed her mother's care from a distance, organizing local help and scheduling regular check-ins. At the same time, Jamie took on more responsibilities at home, ensuring that Mia could focus on her mother without worry.

One evening, as they prepared dinner together in their cozy kitchen, Mia broached a topic on her mind. "Jamie, these past weeks have made me realize how crucial it is to have solid plans for any situation," she said, stirring the sauce on the stove as Jamie chopped vegetables beside her. "Maybe it's time we considered setting up more structured support systems for ourselves and our families."

Jamie nodded, placing the chopped vegetables into a bowl. "I agree," he replied thoughtfully. "It's important to be prepared. Perhaps we could investigate additional insurance or set aside a fund for emergencies?"

Mia was touched by his proactive approach. "That sounds like a good plan," she said, smiling over at him. "Being prepared could reduce the stress when unexpected things happen."

The crisp air and early nightfall brought a sense of calm and introspection as autumn turned to winter. Mia and Jamie often spent evenings wrapped in blankets on their balcony, sipping hot cocoa and discussing everything from future dreams to everyday trivialities. These moments were simple yet profoundly meaningful, encapsulating the essence of their life together.

During one such evening, as they watched the city lights flicker like distant stars, Jamie turned to Mia, his expression serious yet filled with love. "Mia, do you remember the night of the gala, right before all the challenges started?" he asked, his breath visible in the cool air.

Mia nodded, remembering the night vividly. "Of course, how could I forget?"

Jamie took her hand, his grip warm and reassuring. That night, I was so focused on what was going wrong that I never got to tell you something important." He paused, searching her eyes. I love you, Mia. My commitment to you has only grown stronger through the ups and downs."

Tears welled up in Mia's eyes as she squeezed his hand back. "I love you too, Jamie. These months have shown me that no matter what we face, we can get through it together."

Their conversation drifted into plans for the upcoming holidays, a time they intended to spend surrounded by friends and family, celebrating the love and resilience that had defined their year.

As Mia and Jamie finalized their plans for the holiday gathering, they infused each decision with the warmth and love they shared. Their home, already a haven of their combined tastes and memories, would soon be adorned with festive decorations, echoing their joy and gratitude. The preparation for the holidays was not just about celebrating the season but about marking the success of their journey through adversity, a testament to the strength of their partnership.

The night before their guests were due to arrive, Mia found herself reflecting on the past year. It had brought unexpected challenges and profound growth, weaving a tapestry of experiences that colored their life together in new and vibrant shades. As she looked around their living room, transformed for the festive season with lights and garlands, she felt a profound connection to every moment that led them here.

Jamie joined her, wrapping an arm around her shoulders, his presence comforting. "Thinking about the last few months?" he asked, his voice soft.

Mia nodded, leaning onto him. "Yes, it's been quite a journey. I feel like we've become stronger, don't you think?"

"I do," Jamie agreed, kissing her forehead. "It's been challenging, but I wouldn't change a thing. Every step, every decision, has brought us closer."

The next day, as their loved ones filled their home with laughter and stories, Mia and Jamie shared glances of quiet contentment. This gathering was more than a holiday celebration; it symbolized their life together resilient, filled with love, and ever-growing.

The sounds of celebration faded into a peaceful evening. Mia and Jamie stood together on their balcony, watching the snow fall gently over the city. The soft blanket of white seemed to promise a fresh start, mirroring their new beginning.

Mia and Jamie looked forward to the future, with their relationship becoming stronger and more secure. They had plans to explore, dreams to fulfill, and challenges to face, but they were ready—for all of it together.

BRAIENS

As the dust settled on Mia's journey, she stood at the crossroads of her emotions, facing her deepest desires and fears. Her path had been far from straightforward, but it was through the tangled dance of love, rivalry, and self-discovery that she found clarity and strength. The choices she made were not just about choosing between two hearts, but choosing herself – her dreams, her values, and her happiness.Mia learned that love is not a contest but a shared journey, one where authenticity and respect pave the way for lasting connections. Her journey serves as a reminder that the most meaningful relationships begin with self-love and honesty.

Thank you for joining Mia on this unforgettable adventure. May her story inspire you to follow your heart, embrace your authenticity, and navigate the complexities of love with courage and grace.

With love,

Braiens Trinidad